Clint Faraday Mysteries
#9
Follow the Blood

Clint is called by Sergio Sanchez, a good friend with the Policia Nacional in Bocas del Toro to help with a case of murder among some people he was having some trouble with. The trail leads to another murder, earlier, in Costa Rica. Investigating that leads to yet another in Mexico.

Is it a serial killer of some kind – or is there a very understandable motive?

Contents

About the author

CD Moulton has traveled extensively over much of the world both in the music business, where he was a rock guitarist, songwriter and arranger and in an import/export business. He has been everything from a bar owner to auto salvage (junkyard) manager, longshoreman to high steel worker, orchid grower to landscaper, tropical fish farmer to commercial fisherman. He started writing books in 1983 and has published more than 350 books as of January 1, 2023. His most popular books to date are about research with orchids, though much of his science fiction and fantasy work has proven popular. He wrote the CD Grimes, PI series, and the Det. Nick Storie series, Clint Faraday series, and many other works.

He now resides in Gualaca, Chiriqui, Panamá, where he writes books, plays music with friends, does research with orchids and medicinal plants. He has lately become involved in fighting for the rights of the indigenous people, who are among his closest friends, and in fighting the extreme corruption in the courts and police in Panamá.

He offers the free e-book, *Fading Paradise*, that explains what he has been through because of the corruption.

CD is the discoverer of the Chadam Protocol for curing cancer.

Facebook page Ambrosia peruviana for cancer.

Follow the Blood

<u>*Prologue*</u>

Clint Faraday, retired detective from Florida, USA, laid back in the hammock on his deck over Saigon Bay on Isla Colon in Bocas del Toro, Panamá. He sipped the coffee and waved across to Judi Lum, his attractive nextdoor neighbor. She had known him in Florida and met him again in Bocas. Clint had found her to be very useful in the detective work he sort of fell into in Panamá. She was above average intelligent and had a way to get information from people who didn't know they'd given her any. She could act the perfect airhead around people who didn't know her and seem not to even hear when they said things.

She waved back and went out onto her deck to check the epiphytic plants she, Clint, and their weird musician friend had collected. Dave was a botanist who was working on classification of epiphytic plants in Panamá, mostly orchids, but also with rhipsalis, bromeliads, anthuriums, and so forth.

He called across to ask if she wanted to go out to the Zapatillas, a group of islands in the Bocas del

Toro archipelago. She answered that she had to meet with two of the groups she was active in concerning Bocas Town.

Clint said he didn't really want to go himself. He was just bored.

"That case on the coast out of Chiriqui Grande two weeks ago – and you're bored already? That's not even reasonable!"

Clint laughed. He did get bored easily when he wasn't active. That was a basic reason he got in the PI business here. The police found they could work with him very well, so he was called in on murders and some kinds of fraud.

Speaking of which, his celular buzzed with a call from Sergio, a friend on the police force.

"Clint? Sanchez here.

"Are you free at the moment?"

"What you got, Sergio?"

"A murder. Strange kinds of people. Things not *quite* adding up."

"Where?"

"On the road to Changuinola north about two kilometers from the Ojo de Agua road. They were supposedly run off the road by a truck, but some people who were working on timber close saw it and said there was no truck to run them off.

"It seems the dead one, Wilber Stenson, wasn't using a seat belt. The driver, Mark Stedmann, was. The car went into a tree on the passenger side. It did a lot of damage to that side of the car. Stenson was supposedly thrown into the windshield, where he died almost instantly from severe skull fracture and brain damage."

Clint took that in and said, "And?"

"The wound wasn't from that flat a surface. The blood has been smeared onto the windshield in a strange manner."

"Hmm.'Has been smeared' on the glass?"

"Uh-huh. I didn't let on that we third-world pretend Keystone Kops would even note such things."

"You watch too many of those old movies," Clint accused with a laugh. "Almirante?"

"I'll have the truck at the water taxi."

"I'll come over in my own boat. At the end?"

"Fine."

Clint sighed, then told himself he said he was bored, so don't complain if someone has something to break the boredom. He called to Judi to say he was on the way to the mainland and didn't know when he would get back. Keep an eye on things.

"Case?"

"Looks like it."

"Matt! Be careful!"

"You watch too many old ... TV shows, too."

She laughed.

Clint locked up the place and climbed into his boat. Next stop, Almirante.

Sergio had the police truck waiting. The driver, Amos Tomas, said that Sergio was waiting at the accident-that-was-no-accident scene. He arrived with a lot of traffic backed up while the tow-truck pulled the car onto the road to be carried in a slidebed to the police compound, such as it was.

Sergio showed Clint a long series of digital photos of just about every inch of the scene. That was a great thing about a 4G card. They could literally take a couple thousand pictures.

The blood on the windshield was almost an obvious smear. The closeups of the head wounds showed Clint he had been killed with a baseball bat or something like one. Very obviously, also, was that no flat windshield could produce those wounds.

Clint took a quick look into the car. The photos showed the crash bag on the driver's side had deployed. There wasn't one on the passenger side of that model. The passenger seatbelt was in the withdraw. There was a picture of the mechanism of the seat belt that showed it was damaged. The belt couldn't be used. The papers showed the car was a rental, so that was a very deliberate bit of damage.

Stedmann was a fairly large bullish and slightly fat man, maybe six two or three and three hundred ten pounds. He had dark medium length hair and brown eyes. He was wearing reading glasses in some pictures, Clint had noticed.

Sergio pointed to one picture of him with the hair partly in the sun and partly in shade. It was obviously dyed.

Clint singled out a picture that showed him from a slightly back angle.

"Wig," Clint said and pointed to the hair just above the right ear. The color difference showed plainly on one spot.

Sergio grinned. "A small bit of alcohol when I dabbed some on the cut ear. It didn't look right to me at the time."

Clint was always impressed by the quiet subtle way Sergio carried on an investigation. The very professional and complete way.

"Steddman has been taken to the hospital for observation, but the air bag and belt left him with no injuries. He scratched the ear deliberately, I am sure, to cause us to believe that he was slightly injured. He complained that his back and neck hurt. Sometimes he would favor the right arm, sometimes the left...."

"So he wasn't in any pain," Clint agreed. "I think I should speak with the poor guy to be sure he isn't too seriously hurt."

"Yes, please. I am to return to Changuinola immediately. Now that the automobile is on the way, my job is done here. You are requested by the Policia Nacional to assist in traduciendo. Mr. Stedmann does not speak very well the Spanish."

"And you don't speak English."

"Not that Mr. Stedmann knows."

Clint and Sergio got into the police truck with several of the accident scene investigators. Sergio got reports that there was nothing wrong with the car before the crash. Everything was functioning properly.

"Stedmann says he was run off the road by a truck. One of the dirt haulers that come regularly along this part of the road. Testigos state very plainly that there was no truck. It was at seven twelve when it was reported by Stedmann as having occurred within a very few minutes. Less than three, according to him. The trucks do not move before seven thirty. They belong to the company or the nation and are not taken to the homes of the drivers, as the independent truckers do. I have checked with the man who watches the Ojo de Agua project trucks and find there were none other than those on the road from there and they would have to have come from there to run Mr. Stedmann off the road.

"I did not immediately arrest Mr. Stedmann because I know how you work on these things and know you will want to investigate. All such investigations by yourself have proven very helpful to my department in the past. This is a way to have you volunteer without necessity of my requesting formally."

"Oh, why?"

"Because I seem to remember that the friend of Mr. Stedmann, Mr. Oliver Haverton, who Mr. Stedmann listed as a contact upon entering Panamá, was involved in a fatal accident in Costa Rica a week or so ago."

Clint nodded. Sergio was probably the only officer in the area who would automatically remember such details.

They got to Changuinola and went to the police station. Sergio would want Clint to have all the information available before meeting Stedmann. He would supply any information about the group traveling together and the contacts listed by all of them when they arrived in Panamá. Stedmann was in a group looking for investment in supply-side construction materials and machinery. They owned a semi-large dealership in the states and had several exclusive contracts with heavy equipment manufacturers.

Gloria and Wilber Stenson were mostly in plastic and aluminum materials.

Donald Wentworth was in fastening materials. ("Like what?" Clint asked. Sergio handed him papers. Nails, special glues, window bracket holders, acrylic glues, and other such things.) His wife, Wanda, had died a month and a half ago in Mexico from some kind of infection. Clint raised an eyebrow and went on.

Harry and Faith Richards. Molding and forms for concrete or composites.

Ben and Lilian Banks. Steel materials. (Rerod, security doors, etc.)

Anne Haverton, electrical. Her husband, Oliver, was deceased in a whitewater rafting accident in Costa Rica. Their contacts were mostly legitimate large construction companies. Fanny Martinez, Changuinola, was listed as a friend who was supplying habitations. Francisco Arauz was a friend of the Banks. Arturo Serano was a friend of Anne Sanders and her local lawyer. Enrique and Eladio Flores, lawyers and close friends of Stedmann.

Not a lot that was unusual – except that this was the third death among that group in two months and they kept on with the business trip?

"What information can you get about Haverton from Costa Rica?"

"Very little. It was a supposed accident in a river near Nicaragua. The question was why such an accident could happen there. There are many rafters in worse seasons and there has never been a fatal accident there. They listed it as a probably unfortunate accident that happened because the man was drinking too heavily to be on such an adventure." Sergio took a couple of pages from a file and handed them to Clint. They said almost exactly that.

"Know anything about the death in Mexico?"

"Other than that it was in Oaxaca and was the result of an infection, no. It seems the group was the same as here, except Stedmann and Faith Richards weren't along then. A man called Frank Carlysle and a woman called Georgia Manson were with them. They went back to the states, Texas, and Stedmann joined the others there for the rest of the trip."

Clint nodded and asked for permission to call the Costa Rican police for information. Sergio said to make any calls he felt were necessary, but they wouldn't tell him anything.

Which was true. They seemed to have an attitude.

Clint sighed.

"Will you follow the money trail on this one, as they say in the movies?"

Clint nodded, then shook his head. "I think it'll be more productive to follow the blood. I don't like the looks of this.

"Serg, this could be some kind of serial killer. They all have a lot of money, I think. This may be some nut killing off people to show he's smarter than the cops or something as strange. It would be Stedmann, but that would mean he didn't kill ... I don't get it."

"I think I'd like to see what kind of contract they have among themselves. It could prove interesting and informative."

"I can't argue that one! It could be behind the whole mess – or not."

"Whatever. I have to go to interview Stedmann now. Would you be so kind as to volunteer to traducir?"

Clint gave him the finger. They went to the truck.

"This is Donald Wentworth and this is Lilian Banks," Stedmann introduced. "They're traveling with our little group and came to see what they could do to help. Our little trip seems jinxed."

Clint and Sergio shook hands and gave their names. Sergio asked Clint, in Spanish, to please translate what was said, as his English was bad. Clint noted that Lilian seemed to understand Spanish, so said, "Glad to. You don't speak Spanish?"

"I speak only a very little," Lilian answered. "I haven't heard Mark say anything past `cerveza' and `buenos Dias' and that kind of thing."

Clint nodded and said Sergio had asked that he translate.

"First, what's the skinny? You hurt or just shaken up by this?"

"I'm alright, except I'll have some muscle pain for

a couple of days and have to be careful about my neck," Stedmann replied. "I guess I just lucked out. My number's not up quite yet.

"I tend to fatalism. I think, when it's your time to go, there's nothing you can do about it. If it isn't your time, it isn't."

"No muy serioso," Clint said to Sergio.

"What, as exactly as you can remember it, happened?" Clint asked.

"I don't know. I was driving toward – David, actually. We have an appoin ... great Scott! Lilian, please call Jorge Franciso and tell him why we aren't getting to David right about now!"

Lilian looked shocked and went out.

"Anyhow, we were talking about a big job a company in David's doing that has connections with the project here – we supply all kinds of materials and equipment for large construction jobs, you see. This is a working vacation for us. We've come all the way down through Central America.

"We were right there at that curve and a Walker sixteen – that's a dirt hauler truck – came across the center right at us. I went toward the side of the road. The wheel dropped of into a soft rut or something. I remember yelling to hold on, then nothing until I came to with the car having that tree ... Ollie seemed dead or definitely in bad shape. I climbed out and called the emergency number. I got woozy for a few minutes. I remember some people coming from the side of the road a little ways back, then the police.

"You know the rest. The officer was there."

"Estas hablando. Un Walker sixteen camion, afuera la calle, no recorder mucho mas."

"Walker diez y seis?" Sergio asked.

"Uh-huh."

"Bueno. Continuar."

"Anything else?" Clint asked.

"That's about it," Stedmann answered. Clint said that's all he remembers.

"Okay," Sergio said with a sigh and a shake of the head. "Es cierto is un Walker diez y seis? Tu conoce problema con esse."

"Are you absolutely certain it was a Walker sixteen?" Clint asked. "There aren't a lot of those here. Too big for that stretch of road. Too heavy. It must have been empty and traveling too fast for the conditions. Maybe they can find it pretty fast."

"Well, it was a sixteen or twelve, but I'm pretty sure it was sixteen. It's possible the fact it was barreling at me and I exaggerated it in my mind, but I really don't think so. It was awfully fast."

"Mas cierto. Possiblemente is doce, pero el no crea."

"Gracias por su testimonio."

"Thanks. He'll make the report."

"We have to go to David. Today, if possible."

"Necessario esta por David hoy, si posible."

"Otros si, pero el es por aqui hasta reportar. Hoy? Posiblemente, pero probablamente una dia."

"The others can go. You have to stay around to formalize your statement. Possibly today, but probably tomorrow."

"I can live with that. Thanks."

They left. Lilian Banks was talking to a man in the waiting room. She introduced Harry Richards. Harry said this was terrible! They were cursed!

Clint said life seemed that way at times. They certainly had their share of bad luck.

He went on to the station with Sergio. "I think I want to go to Costa Rica and poke around a bit. It shouldn't take long."

Sergio said he'd have him taken to the border and slipped through without delay. He wouldn't be delayed coming back because he would be carrying National Police papers. He took a form out and filled it in, then signed it and had a man take it to the court to have a stamp put on it. Clint went to Almirante in the police truck and got his backpack with fresh clothes and such, then was back in Changuinola for the papers, then to Sixola, then into Costa Rica, where he got a bus to Limon. He went to a town called Piedras (rocks) near the Nicaraguan border. He got a room in the only pension, ate a good meal at the restaurant and went to one of the three local bars to ask a few questions.

"Los gringos quien esta por whitewater. Uno morio'."

"I speak English and book all the whitewater trips," the tall thin man said. "Octavio Arrenz."

"Clint Faraday. I have to know about that trip and why anyone, drunk or not, would die along that stretch."

"Suspicious as hell to me, too. No one was drunk when they left here. It wasn't but about four kilometers down the river. I don't think anyone could drink much crossing the first rill. That meant he got too drunk to navigate in ten minutes? Bullshit!"

"Yeah. They had another socalled accident in Panamá. Another one's dead."

"That Faith woman there? The looker. Bimbo body, but MENSA mind?"

"Think she's got her sexy ass in it?" Clint had never seen her. This was the kind of information he needed.

"Well, she acts like an airhead's airhead, but things slip into it that make it very damned sure obvious that she's smart as all hell. She can't resist getting a zinger in on some of the others when she gets the chance. That takes a really quick fucking mind.

"I don't know if she was flirting. It seemed like it."

"Promising looks, then she's insulted if you take her up on it. Too many like that anymore."

"Yeah. I got my rusty ass burned enough that I act like I don't get the fucking hint."

Clint bought another beer. Two bucks apiece here, sixty cents in Panamá.

"I have some suspicions. Things happened in other places that they let little things slip about.," Clint confided.

"Something damned sure as all hell happened in Mexico or Guatemala! I heard that Lily woman saying she was worried that they might get the same kind of thing in the countries down here," he replied. "We're all so backward and prehistoric in these rathole places. Fucking enough to make you want to smack her in the fucking puss!"

"Too many gringos like that. We all have to live with what people think of us because of them."

He nodded. They chatted for a little while and Clint started talking to an attractive girl. She turned out to be very interested in him, too. Fifty bucks worth of interested.

Clint told her he didn't screw around on his girlfriend. Maybe some other time. She lost interest. Clint went to the pension and to bed.

What to do now? He had the information he needed from Costa Rica.

Clint looked over the papers from the court. He could go anywhere with government sanction from Mexico to Brazil.

So he'd go to Mexico. Oaxaca. He called for a flight and took a bus, then a cab to the airport in San Jose'. He was landing in Oaxaca at dusk. Seemed like that's when he got anywhere.

This would be different. He couldn't get his information in a little local pub in Oaxaca.

Good lord! He didn't tell Sergio he was going to Mexico!

He called and Sergio said he suspected that when Clint didn't come back. Stedmann was allowed to go to David about four o'clock. Judi Lum said she had some information about things that Clint might be interested in knowing.

Clint called her. She said there was some talk in Bocas Town about the supposed accident on the Changuinola road. It seemed Dona Sanchocho's husband, Juan, was cutting nispero not five hundred meters from the socalled accident. The man in the car had lied when he said there was a truck to run him off the road. There was no truck. He told the police that and gave a statement, but they let the driver go. Probably paid off.

"Paid off? Sergio?" Clint asked.

"Exactly what I told them. There's no way anyone

paid off Sergio Sanchez.

"I figure you're investigating that fatal accident? That's why your phone's turned off?"

"Yes, I'm investigating it. No, my phone's not turned off. I was in Costa Rica yesterday and am in Mexico now. Home tomorrow, I hope.

"See what the scuttle's about among that bunch, Okay?"

"Other than that one of them is a sex-bomb, I haven't heard much. I'll listen and suggest."

"Thanks, Judi. This is kind of strange. I'll get back as soon as I can."

"Clint? Manny's got the connections that could help in Mexico."

"Thanks! I hadn't thought of that. If I can't find anything on my own I'll call him."

They chatted a bit, then Clint went to a good restaurant for a mixed mariscos dish something like paella. He would go to the police station in the morning.

"I did not believe what they told me, about her cutting herself on some shells in the ocean in Mar Vista and that it became infected during the drive to here, then she took some antibiotics from a farmacia, but she wasn't conscious much in the hospital here. Her nurse, Carmencita Vilas, said she kept trying to tell her something, but she didn't make sense and she didn't speak Spanish enough to make her understand what she was saying," Sgt. Mario Cestas read from the report. "That was from Officer Cortez, who makes out police reports when someone dies."

"Thanks," Clint said. "Can I find him to ask a question or two?"

"He will be at ... (he looked at a work sheet) the morgue. He is talking with the family of a lady who died of too much alcohol. It is a great problem here."

He explained where to find the morgue and gave him a short note that Clint was authorized to make inquiries into past deaths. Clint found the morgue and waited outside until Cortez finished counseling the family.

"I need to know whatever you remember about this case." He handed Cortez the report. Cortez raised an eyebrow.

"You said you didn't believe them?"

"They seemed to be placing a false face. What has happened?"

"Two more in that group have died under suspicious circumstances."

He nodded and sighed.

"That woman who looks like a movie queen was impatient that they had to get to Guatemala to meet another partner while two of the group had to get back to Texas? Her business partner and friend had died the night before and it was an inconvenience, no more? They had an infection like that, a resistant strain of staphylococcus, and bought some expired antibiotic cream from a local farmacia? They had already made arrangements for the body to be sent back to Texas for cremation? A prepaid funeral and cremation is rather common today, but the family and friends generally go to the funeral, at the least.

"The *husband*, `Donny', they called him, only was concerned about some kind of contract she was supposed to sign and was wondering if perhaps he could sign it with a copy of her death certificate?

"I made the certificate to say she had died of the staphylococcus infection, but there were serious questions as to how and why she became infected and was not treated immediately. I noted on the report that I didn't believe them."

"The nurse said she tried to tell her something?"

"I ... yes, I noted that. You may speak with her. I will translate."

"Yo hablo poco bien el espaniol. Mil gracias por sus consideracion."

"Muy buenos dias."

Clint looked up the nurse. She wasn't on duty, but the receptionist gave him her address and celular number. He called her and arranged to meet her for lunch in the Buena Vista Hotel restaurant.

"Miss Vilas? I'm, er, llamame Clint."
"Cita. Que desea?"

(translated) "I have to find what I can about a Wanda Wentworth who died of a staph infection here a couple of weeks ago. You reported that she tried to tell you something? Can you remember anything about it at all?"

"I understood only a few words. `Killed Sammy' and `Houston Texas' and `Veronica'. I think she was saying she had killed someone or that someone there had killed someone named Sammy. I think Veronica was ... I don't know.

"Clint, they are very strange and cold people who talk only of money and contracts while one of their friends and partners is dying right in front of them. Why was that resistant staphylococcus even in this part of Mexico? There had been two cases in Mexico City last year. Never here or in Mar Vista. They bought some antibiotic cream in a pharmacy that was expired and didn't seek a doctor when it didn't work? They drove all the way here with her unconscious part of the time in one of their cars?

"Excuse the vulgarity. Bullshit!"

"Two more have died. Both under what we call questionable circumstances. I'm trying to find what the hell is going on. I don't personally care if they kill each other off to the last one. I want to know why."

She nodded. "Perhaps Mario of the police will be able to find some information about Sammy or Veronica. His cousin is working for the police department in Houston, Texas."

"Thanks, Cita. This is a big help. I'd ask for a date if I didn't have to go. You're a beautiful woman."

She laughed. "You would have to first garner permission from my husband!"

They chatted a few minutes, then Clint headed back to the police station.

"You can get the info?" Clint asked.

"I can try. I think, yes," Mario answered. "I was more than a little concerned and have asked that Harry find what he can, but there was no urgency. Your papers indicate that I may treat this as an official inquiry. Texas is cooperative in many things."

He used the computer to call Houston, ask for official connection with Sgt. Harold Guterez, and explained what he wanted if he could find any connection with the people on the list he gave two weeks ago.

I have already found that the name, Frank Carlysle, was probably who is in question. He was killed in a mugging a month ago. The fourteenth. There wasn't any way to find who killed him. He ran errands for the SfTSpec, for whom he was delivering a package when killed. Veronica could possibly be Veronica Mayfield, the girlfriend of a man in the group who wasn't there in Oaxaca. Markus Stedmann. She has disappeared three days later. It is reported by the woman who runs the apartment building where she was staying that she is hiding from someone, perhaps a mean suitor or past boyfriend. There is no more I can discover.

"The SfTSpec?" Clint asked.

"I think perhaps the name of their company. I will see." He ran a Google search on the name. It was a company registered to that group and six others. "I imagine it will take perhaps three days to gather all the information about the company and the partners from Texas. I will give you the internet code for my machine and will arrange to transfer any details to your own computer.

"I must say that computers have proven a great boon to police work, in some ways. So much is there. It is merely a matter of knowing where to find it."

Clint was about to ask him to check further on that company, but was, apparently, anticipated. He used the computers quite a bit, but this was the first time he actually saw an official police investigation use Google! Now he would continue the search and send him the results.

Hell, the information is there. Use it.

He said his thanks and goodbyes and headed for the airport. He would get to Panamá City at eleven the following day.

He went to the hotel and got a good night's sleep, after calling Sergio with what he had learned.

"Well, I've learned enough that you can freeze their movements," Clint told Sergio. "It would be a lot of lawyers and affidavits and such in the states. Here, you just arrest them."

"I'll have an order that they may not leave Panamá City until the investigation here is completed."

"I think maybe I'll just sit back and wait for the information to be sent to me. It'll take a few days."

"How long can you hold them?"

"For as long as the investigation takes. I will simply tell them they may remain free, but will be arrested and held in carcel should they be so stupid as to try to leave the country. It would be seen as a sign of guilt by the courts."

"I can use a day or two for fishing and such. Going out of Panamá tires the hell out of me."

"I will inform you if there is any progress or detail that should come to your attention."

"Thanks, Sergio."

They talked a bit more, then Clint went to his place, spent what was left of the day with Judi and Ben, a neighbor. Dave was in town, so they went to El Ultimo Refugio to see him play with some of the local musicians. It was a pleasant night, but Clint went home early.

In the morning Clint went to all the regular stops to talk with the regulars. Manny and family (Manny Mathews, actually Marko Bocinni, a retired godfather Clint helped find a way to raise his family without interference by the old mob in California) came to shop a bit for groceries. Clint told him about the case. Manny said he would put out a notice for information. Clint said he would ask if it came to that point. He may get it without the hassle.

"I seem to have a nagging feeling that I know something about that bunch. The name of the company seems familiar, somehow. Maybe it's connected, but not very strongly."

They talked about a lot of things, then Clint went out to visit friend who lived at The Bluffs, then he went fishing for about an hour for his supper. It was a pleasant laid-back day in paradise.

He went to Isla Carenero to see how friends there were doing that evening until about eleven, then home to grab a good sleep. He got up at six in the morning, back to his normal schedule.

Manny had sent a bit of new information on the computer. It seemed there were some unanswered questions about that company and some of the people who ran it. Someone had disappeared a couple of years ago and there was a stink, but nothing was ever proven on any of them. They claimed Robert Mesmer had absconded with a large sum they couldn't file charges on through legal channels – which meant they were what's commonly called "Unreported income" in those circles.

There were some things to be learned from Atlantic City and Chicago. He would have someone dig a bit for his own curiosity.

This thing was stretching out into the past. Clint decided he would try to find what had happened to anyone in that company from its inception. He wanted to see exactly what this was about. Was it some kind of survivor's club, where one or two of them were trying to see that they were the survivors? Were more taken in along the way?

Clint remembered a book he'd read long ago called *The Hunter's Club*. It was a group who decided hunting big game was getting boring. The standard targets had no way to fight back. A shot from a high-powered rifle from 200 yards wasn't much of a challenge. They decided the only "worthwhile" game was man. The reactions of these people showed it may actually be some sick kind of game they were playing.

Sergio called and said the evidence they had now, including the witnesses and type of physical damage, was enough to convict Stedmann. Should he proceed in that, or wait?

"Sergio, there's something strange and sinister

about this thing. Let's take a time out and watch them. I'm gathering some evidence that this may be ... what it's beginning to look like. That's very scary."

"What do you mean?"

"Let's see how far back this thing goes, if we can."

"We know about Costa Rica. We can't prove anything there except the connection. One and one is still two."

"Depends on the math you're using. It can be a lot of things. I don't think just two."

"Two we know about. It is our basic pattern."

"Three, then. Mexico's more certain than Costa Rica."

"You know a lot more than I do about this. They aren't going anywhere. We'll take, as you say, a time out."

Clint called Manny when Sergio hung up to ask if anything new had come up. Manny said there seemed to be some kind of attempt to hide that company from public view.

They chatted about various things, then Clint went to his computer. A Google search followed by a Yahoo! search proved to be much more interesting. SfTSpec was a company started, according to three hours of searching, in 1998 by a group of people who owned businesses having to do with construction and home repairs. It also had a member who had a heavy equipment parts distributor company. There were twenty original members. Clint did a search on all of them to find little except that Susan and Kyle Long, who owned a lumber mill and a chain of retail outlets for building materials had died in a car wreck when their brakes failed in the mountains in Colorado in December of 1998. There was some suspicion the car had been purposely damaged, but nothing was found in the investigation. There was no apparent motive for anyone in the area to want to harm them. The possessions were in a corporate holding, so no individual would profit very greatly. All the members of the corporation were independently wealthy.

Clint sat back to think. There were a number of questions to ask a computer from a number of angles. It was a time-consuming task. (God! He was thinking in those terms?)

Well, onward and upward. Or downward. Or sideways. How many?

He had Wilber Stenson. One, and he had Oliver Haverton and Wanda Wentworth. Wanda wasn't in the corporation. Was that important? Did it take motive away from anyone?

What was the name Sergio's cousin sent? Frank Carlysle?

A check showed he was just a delivery service. A deeper check showed there were a couple of complaints against him for opening packages ... so that could well be motive. He found something in a package.

What about Wanda Wentworth? They said no one seemed in the least concerned that she was dead. She found something, too? Hubby Dear left some odd papers around or something?

Clint checked Texas and Mexico to try to get a connection that would involve her with something else.

Acapulco. James Smart, an original member of the group and his lover, John Truman, had died in a boating accident two weeks before on their way from California to Acapulco in 2007. From what could be pieced together from the evidence there must have been a gas leak and a spark set it off when they anchored out from Acapulco and came in the dingy to spend two days there. When they returned and started the engine, the boat exploded in a manner that indicated a poorly vented engine compartment. No mention was made of the company. There was no connection anyone knew about. Unfortunate accident.

How many others? One and one was now six. Time to dig deeper into this.

Who was close when all of the deaths occurred?

That couldn't be traced easily. Some of it was more than ten years ago.

All he could do was try. He called Manny and told

him what he'd found to date. Manny said any connection could lead to other connections. They had something more to work with.

He decided to see what he could about the company. Maybe the founders' list would give him a clue. He still didn't know if it was one, two, the whole group, or what.

Donald Fieldman, Harold and Faith Richards, John Truman, James Smart, Mark Stedmann, Eugene Williams, Oliver and Anne Haverton, Donald Wentworth, Bart Green,Georgia and Samuel Hicks, Barbara Manson, Lonnie Gene Michaels, Susan and Kyle Long, Lucille Baldwin, Samuel Green, Wilber Stenson.

Were Samuel and Bart Green related?

Not according to what he could find. Green was certainly not an uncommon name.

SfTSpec. Where did the name come from?

He checked over the list. Stedmann, Stenson. Smart.

F? Not capitalized? A first name? Frank? There was a Donald Fieldman.

T? Truman?

If it was Stenson or Smart and Frank Carlysle – *not* a member. It wasn't him. That left only Fieldman. If it was Smart or Stenson, Fieldman, and Truman, two of them were dead.

Was Fieldman dead?

That would take some checking.

Clint worked until five thirty, then he and Judi
went out for a relaxing night on the town.

"Well, Sergio, it seems your one and one is two is now one and one is six – and growing!"

"I have traced a few things about Stedmann. There is not much of a trail. He is in the company with the others here. He has been involved with another person, this Faith Richards, in another business deal, earlier, with a man called Donald Fieldman. It was about some kind of stock exchange or something and in the mid-nineties.

"There are a lot of almost-dead ends in this one."

"Tell me about it!"

"I just did."

Clint gave him the finger. They chatted a bit more, but there wasn't much new. Clint wanted to know something about Fieldman, but simply couldn't find much. The name had pages on Google etc, but nothing that would make a positive connection with the one he was looking for.

That's the trouble with such search engines. You can usually find hundreds, even thousands of references to a certain person or thing, but simply knowing the name you want isn't enough to concentrate the search.

Clint narrowed it a bit by limiting the search to

Texas. There were only fifty six pages on Donald Fieldman Texas. Clint followed twenty or so reference hyperlinks and learned virtually nothing more.

Sergio called and said he'd found a little bit. Markus J. Stedmann from Texas had connections on the web with a Susan and Kyle Long and a Faith Newsom, who was now Faith Richards. He was going to check on the Longs. They were in the company.

Clint agreed and went back to the computer to look for Susan and Kyle Long.

Uh-oh! Deceased in a fire that had trapped them in their home in Carmel, California, in 2004. It was determined that the fire was "probably" arson, but was done so cleverly that it was not provable.

One and one now equaled eight.

Were there more?

Probably. This was one sick bunch of people.

Well, now it could be pieced together in an odd sort of way. Maybe one eighty degrees wrong, but something to investigate.

Faith Newsom had business dealing with Mark Stedmann. Was that the start? Maybe they were working together ever since, which meant they would probably have been together before.

Then why wasn't Newsom part of the company name? Did the company name have anything or nothing to do with people's names?

Assume the company was named for the ones who started it. The purpose of the company was first ... this part would depend on who the starters were. Stenson, Smart, Truman were dead. Was that because they started the group and it got away from them?

If it was Stedmann, it still got away from Truman, so until he knew who "f" was he didn't have much. If it was Fieldman he had to know something about him. That was the really hard part.

Past that. Get your mind into order and let the tangents go until you have something to use to investigate.

The company was a survivor's club that made them kill each other off ... this wasn't making sense! If that was the deal, why travel together? Was it sicker than he even dared guess?

Clint got in his boat and went to Almirante and to the police station to talk with Sergio.

"Sergio, can you tag Stedmann and leave the others out of it?"

"I think so. Why?"

"Because this is one chilling sick mess! I can't figure it but one way and that is so sick ... I wonder if Stedmann'll give himself up to protect the others to kill off each other? I wonder if part of it's that if you get caught you're out and the others must be kept in the clear, no matter what?

"God! This has to be the sickest deal I ever heard

of! Even if I'm wrong on two thirds of it, it's still sicker than anything I've run across in fifty years as a detective. Serg, I think this is just a game to keep them from getting bored."

"They don't seem to go for torture or any of that. What do you mean?"

"I'm out to kill you in any way I can. The whole bunch of you. Vice versa for the whole bunch of us. If I get caught I'm obligated to protect you and the game. This is sport and nothing personal. We're out to kill each other, but we can still be friends.

"That's the best scenario. Part of it has to do with ... I can't figure anything this sick. I try to put myself in the mind of anyone I'm after. I don't have a reference. I can't put myself into that frame. It's either completely sane and logical from an unbelievably cold point of view or we have a whole bunch of totally insane crackpots.

"Serg, if there are that many, how did they find each other? The number means it's some kind of cult thing or something – but there's no evidence of that kind of activity."

"TV movies," Sergio replied. "They watch all those violence and horror things and see that as a part of life."

"They're all too old for that kind of influence in ... maybe not, but it would be the Manson ... I wonder. Is Barbara Manson her real name or did she ... we have to know a lot about that one. That may be our big connecting clue."

Sergio pointed to the comp on his desk. "It's personal. The office computer is that one on the desk with the printer. Maybe you can ... I'll give you her passport number. That's usually the best way to trace name changes and so forth. If you have trouble with information from the states – and you will, coming from Panamá – you can use the official connection with your consul. They cooperate when the rest of your government won't."

"Uh-oh?"

"Some kind of deal where your FBI wants us to arrest some people who they say are drug dealers. We know some of them definitely aren't. We aren't about to start arresting people because the big bad powerful United States gives us orders. They can fuck off, if you ask me!"

Sergio never used maldiciones. Clint could see he was really getting hot about it. That was the atmosphere George W. planted. It got better for a few months after the election, now was getting as bad or worse.

"It's not the gringos here. It's the ones who think being powerful in the states makes them powerful here," Sergio said. "Most of the gringos here are very good people. It's like that woman in Haiti in one of your cases (*Comedy of Terrors*) who thought the fact she could terrorize Haitians and Jamaicans into doing anything she demanded by using their fear of voodoo meant Panamanians would do anything she demanded. You saw exactly how far that got her! Panamanians don't give a shit about some witch woman in Haiti or about the all-powerful FBI.

"Maybe you can find something there. I'll check on anything I can. Will you want me to arrest Stedmann?"

"Might as well. Maybe I can get him to talk. I'm sure he thinks he's gotten away with a hell of a lot. He's going to be the type to brag."

Sergio nodded.

Barbara Manson was Barbara Manson. Not even a relative of Charles Manson. It wasn't an alias. Clint decided to crossreference everyone dead he knew about and to try to find if any of the others were dead.

Four hours and he found that Lucille and Edward Baldwin had died in Nevada when they were camping near a river on vacation three years and two months ago. They ate some sandwiches that were contaminated with botulism and were too far from medical aid and too sick to climb the mountain to their car. It was a very fast-acting form of the food poisoning and there was fear for a while that the strain might be in the area, but they apparently brought it with them in some mayonnaise that they had inadvertently left unrefrigerated. The cooler was warm when they were found the next day by rafters.

1+1 = 9. How many more?

"Sergio, I'm on my way to Panamá City to see what I can learn from Stedmann. I don't think he's the head ... person. It could be Faith Richards and he was conned into it by her or it could be almost anyone. There's nothing to say that whoever's running the game is a member of that company, though I think so."

"That's something I was going to point out. It may be some evil nut from outside who set it up for personal reasons we can't hope to determine or understand.

"Well, there is nothing in the law that says we must understand the motives of criminals, only that we must prosecute them, particularly where violence is part of the equation. Murder is, very certainly, considered a violent crime – even when it is with a narcotic that would make it an almost pleasant death. Definitions, you see."

"By any definition this is one weird situation and one weird bunch of, I guess you would have to call them people. Definitions."

The radio called for Sergio, who answered.

"Sergio Sanchez? I am Sgt. Flacco. You asked that we report on the movements of a group of tourists traveling on business visas when we arrested one of them?"

"Yes. The Stedmann case."

"They seem very strange people. We arrest a man who is in their group and who has been charged with killing another in that group and they seem to want to complain that it makes for a very inconvenient pause in their business dealings! They seem to think he was very stupid to get caught!

"A woman, very beautiful, a Faith Richards, said that Stedmann thought this country wouldn't see what had happened and it was most inconsiderate of him to do anything that obvious. They are not sane, I think. They are such cold examples of the human race!"

"Clint Faraday, who is known and who works with us in many cases as a consultant and investigator, will come there to speak with Mr. Stedmann. It will be greatly appreciated by the department if you will offer him all cooperation that is legal in handling this matter."

"Yes. Okay, he's gone for a minute." Clint raised an eyebrow and Sergio said the captain was in the room. Flacco was a good friend, then into the microphone, "We also think there is something very weird about those people, Jorge. Outside the legal jargon (Sergio using a word like jargon'?) we think they are a bunch of homicidal maniacs!"

"Yeah, Sanch. I sort of got that impression. We'll

help any way we can. Clint Faraday is a name known and respected here."

He whispered, "Capitan Nuncio!" then went back to the "official" voice. "We will offer any and all cooperation we may legally tender to your operative, Mr. Faraday.

"Base clear."

"Weirder yet," Clint said. Sergio nodded and looked very grim.

Clint went back to his house in Bocas Town, spent some time with Judi – who said a girl at the garden club had a brother who went to Los Angeles for an engineering firm to find someone who could help with the oil refinery and had met the man who had died in the car crash on the Changuinola road. He was with a man they called "Don" and who was a very managerial type who wanted to run everything, so he went to another firm to find an engineer. Did that help?"

"You know, it just might!

"Judi, you can come up with information we couldn't find in four days of research with all the modern methods! How do you *do* it?"

"Practice, practice, practice.

"Clint, you want to find things and ask in ways that make people suspicious about why you ask. You don't do it with the Indios because you know damned well they'll clam. I inject a word or so into a conversation and move on. They say things and I act like it's interesting, but only as an anecdote, then pass on. They usually forget they said anything. It's a psychological approach."

"Whatever, now you've pointed out something I was doing wrong all along. I think you're a better detective than me!"

"I can get information. You know what to do with it after we have it. I don't."

"We make a hell of a good team, don't we?"

"Sorta. Got to go to the vigilante meeting."

"Why? You don't own a business here."

"Neither does Dave, but they always invite him. I sort of was invited to tag along when I went the first time with him."

"Anyhow, I'll be back as soon as I can. I'll go crazy if I can't find what this crap's about! I think it's a very, very sick game they're playing. Good friends who kill off each other to see who lives longest. I suppose that one's the winner – or something."

Judi shuddered. "As you say, sick, sick, sick."

"Well, you have to admit – it fights boredom!"

She gave him the finger. He laughed, she left, he cleared everything up on the computer to clear up and finish what he could of that and packed things for a couple of days in Panamá City.

He then went to Changuinola for a flight to David. They didn't go to Bocas Town from David anymore.

He stopped in Almirante to discuss things with Sergio. He reported that the group wanted his permission to go on to Colombia to continue their business trip. They were told they could possibly leave in two more days after they gave their testigo declarations.

"They are so damned cold!" Sergio complained. "I think they feel nothing at anytime about anything!"

"That's a pretty good description," Clint agreed. "God! I hate cities!"

"You like David. It is a favorite place to you."

"David isn't like any city I've ever seen. It's ... different. A big town, not a city."

"A town? With high rises, casinos, very fine restaurants, shopping malls?"

"That's what makes it different. It also has very warm and friendly people who have time to say 'Buenos!' and are helpful as anyone can be. It's tranquil, except for a few blocks around Centro. Dave's apartment's five blocks from Centro and it's like a very quiet suburb – except when one neighbor cranks up the stereo until the neighbors complain. Panamanians love noise. The bars are so loud you have to scream at each other across the table. Stores have speakers on the street that almost knock you down when you walk past. It's strange and a little irritating to gringos, but has an odd charm. I only wish they'd play something besides salsa and regaton. I'm sick to death of the same dozen songs over and over again for six years.

"There's very little pollution. There's nowhere near the crime a city of that size always has."

"We like noise. True. It's a part of our culture."

Clint nodded and said he'd call when he had anything. He got a bus to Changuinola and was talking to an Indio friend when they passed the spot of the crash. His cousin was there working on timber when the crash happened and said there was no truck to cause it. Clint said he knew that.

"He told the policia. They didn't do anything. Gringos get away with murder here – and that is not an expression."

"No. They don't. He's been arrested in Panamá and will be convicted of murder," Clint replied. "Pancho, the police act here, in most cases. Gringos or Panamanians. They often are onesided against the indigenos, but that's changing. They're very efficient, but quiet. They don't want publicity, except to an extent that people will know criminality *will* be prosecuted."

"This is true? You know it for a fact?"

"Yeah, Pancho. I'm on my way to Panamá to help with the court to convict Stedmann."

"Then it is well. I will inform my cousin and the others who were there and told the policia."

They chatted a bit more about more pleasant subjects. Clint got to Changuinola and caught the flight to David. He would prefer to take the bus, but this was forty five minutes while the bus was four hours. He was in David five hours to speak with people concerned with this there, then caught the midnight express bus to Panamá City, after visiting the places where he could relax for a few minutes.

He got to Panamá City at eight in the morning and went directly to the police station.

"We spoke a few minutes in Almirante," Clint greeted Stedmann when he was led into the interrogation room. Stedmann studied him for a few seconds.

"So. Now I understand why I'm here. A gringo cop working with the local yokels."

"Don't kid yourself. Sergio saw everything in two minutes at the scene. He called me because of that. They use me with gringos they consider particularly weird. Translator."

"They consider me weird?" It was simply a question. No emotion in it.

"Certainly. You know damned well you are."

He laughed shortly. "I guess I am. We all are, in some ways."

"Gonna tell me what it's about? The game?"

"You figured it's a game?"

"Follow the blood. We know about nine – ten, but Carlysle wasn't a member of the group, only some schnook who had the bad luck to look in a package of yours."

He nodded and looked thoughtful. "And you think we're crazy?"

"Not much doubt, is there?"

"I sometimes wonder why I can't ... that there's a lack in us. We don't react to things like on television. We don't react to anything."

Clint's turn to nod. "It's a strange psychological constitutional condition. I just wonder how the bunch of you found each other."

"We were led together by a friend of Fuh ... of one of us. He set things up because he found life to be incredibly boring. He's a genius, in some ways. He's a control freak who wanted to set something up that he couldn't control after its inception. He wants a challenge."

Clint remembered what Judi said. Don. It wasn't Wentworth, so... "Fieldman. Yeah. Faith is more or less his agent." Clint also noticed that "He wants" – so Fieldman was still among the living.

Stedmann looked shocked, then wary. "It's not so much ... it got away from all of us, but we go on with it. I don't have the least conception of why." Clint let it pass, mostly. He acted like he was thinking of something else, which relaxed Stedmann.

"Boredom. You thought it would put some new excitement in your lives, it did for a little while, now it's just as boring as everything else," he replied, in a disinterested manner.

"Could be. What do you think will happen? Not that I care much. It's just another something that happened. I'm sort of like standing to one side and watching a bad TV flick. Nothing will change, except I'll sit in some cell until I die or something. All of us have millions, but can't even buy one lousy day of difference."

It sounded rehearsed. Clint had read some psychology books when he was first into the detective thing. This was almost like it was a memorized rote passage from one of them. The distached personality. Sociopathic. Good Ol' Stedmann was about to learn something about Panamá ! That kind of psychobabble didn't have much weight in court here. He wouldn't get a term in a psycho ward, then be released in a couple of years as cured.

Would it give him a minute of excitement to learn another plan was flawed by a small detail that could smack him in the puss? Hard?

"That doesn't work here. No bleeding heart, `Oh, The poor dear! He wasn't responsible for what he did because his father molested him when he was just nine years old!' or `His mother cut off the boob too soon,' or that kind of thing. You'll get the max. You might have gotten the minimum sentence, six years, if we didn't find out about the others. The police here don't throw up their hands and say there isn't enough proof like some other countries – for gringos. They'll do it *to* a gringo. We don't kid ourselves about the old `screw the gringo' being alive and well in Panamá."

"Yet you work for them?"

"I work with them. That doesn't apply to the ones of us who live like they have some respect for the people here. Too many gringos have an attitude. They're snobs with a bad attitude and no one's going to appreciate that. This has nothing to do with anything. It's just an explanation about what you misjudged."

"So? What do you expect from me? Some kind of confession to make it easier for you?"

"They don't need any confession. It wouldn't change anything. They have all the proof they need to convict or they wouldn't have arrested you."

"I can see problems in court. They can't prove I wasn't run off the road and crashed."

"Oh, that. They have four witnesses working a couple of hundred meters from there who say there was no truck, plus the traffic coordinators for the Ojo de Agua project have watchers to guarantee that their own fleet doesn't exceed the rules. They note every truck that passes. There weren't any, much less a Walker sixteen. You also have the fact that Stenson was dead before the crash. Baseball bat is the probable cause. The ME states very plainly that the head injuries were absolutely and positively *not* caused by contact with a flat windshield. You're gone for that."

"I guess I'll need a really good lawyer."

"If you find one who'll take your case you'll find

that he or she is definitely not a good lawyer. The good ones refuse unwinnable cases. You aren't allowed a lawyer by law here. This ain't Texas."

He looked at Clint with a deeply thoughtful expression mixed with a bit of fear and/or shock. Maybe Clint had given him a few seconds of emotion, even if it was only fear.

He sighed and nodded. "I'm through talking. I have to think this through. I very seldom make blunders on this order – if what you say is true."

"Your choice. You know damned well it's true. You figured them for a bunch of, as you said, yokels. They're very efficient cops. They do their job and do it well, but shy away from publicity that turns cops into public figures or TV heroes. That always leads to an inflated opinion of themselves that soon turns them into worthless excuses for cops.

"You may be able to get a high-priced lawyer, don't mistake that, but it'll be for the money. He or she or they won't make an iota of difference in your case. Theatrics and tricks don't work in this system. It's more likely to get a lawyer barred from practicing. They do it on TV, of course. It impresses the marks.

"In short, they'll present a huge bill for all the writs and proofs and such they had to research at two or three hundred bucks an hour – and they spent fifty hours this week on your case, alone.

They tell other clients much the same thing, the socalled hours spent determined by how much money you have. They can end up spending a hundred fifty or two hundred hours per week exclusively on individual client's cases. It's hard to relate that to the fact that their clients almost always seem to lose because it was a hopeless case from the first.

"Good luck! You're damned well going to need some!"

He merely looked interested. "And you can help shave some off the sentence if I give you some information." It was a positive statement.

"Not a chance. They don't work that way. If they have you as solid as they have, you don't get any deals. You may be able to get some favors from the court later, after conviction, to make things a little easier. Even that's marginal. The rules are the rules. Martinelli is cracking down hard on corruption, so that's damned iffy. You aren't going to be able to buy a life of ease in the pen here." He started looking through papers in his briefcase.

"I've found that to be true. We couldn't get anything from people we have in the past. They say things are different and we'll have to wait for the next president. They're sure two in a row won't be the same. The next one won't be richer than Midas and will be corruptible. It's the way things have always been here."

"Oh, yeah. That bunch in Changuinola." Clint acted like he was looking for something that wasn't there.

"The Flores were always a source of help in arranging special permits and such. Fanny always came through when it came to avoiding taxes and fees. Give her five hundred bucks and save five thousand."

Clint repressed a smirk and managed to look disinterested. "Well, guess I'll be going. I was just here from personal curiosity, more than anything else."

"I think I'll study a bit of the law here. They let me have my laptop and the laws are all on the net under public property regulations.

"I won't find much to help, huh?"

"Probably the opposite. If you're subject to deeper depression than you're living in anyway I would say not to do it. In your case, I doubt it would make any difference."

He nodded and offered his hand. Clint grinned and shook it. When he left the room he handed the recorder that was sitting right there on the table from the first to the officer and said there were some good evidentiary details about two lawyers and a woman in Changuinola. It was enough to apply as proof of petty corruption and bribery.

"How did you manage that?"

"Judi told me why I never seemed to get straight

answers from people in instances like this. Call it misdirection."

He got a look like this guy thought he was as crazy as Stedmann. He talked with the capitan for a few minutes, then headed for his hotel. He knew the one – ones – he had to check from 'way back. He called Judi to say, "Thanks! It works!"

"You never make any sense. I take it your case is solved?"

"I have the direction to go. I think I'll solve it now."

They chatted a little while, then Clint went to dinner and some talk with people he met. He ran into a girl he had spent time with in Bocas Town, so spent most of the night at her place.

In short, it was a great night!

Clint got into David at four, so went directly to Dave's apartment there instead of the Pension Costa Rica. Dave had given him the keys and wouldn't be in town for a few days. He'd gone to Las Tablas. Clint could use the computer there. It was online and very fast. He'd found what he had to know to dig back to where this started, hopefully. It wasn't going to be easy, but Sergio had given him some ideas.

Manny!

He called Manny Mathews and asked if he had learned anything more. Other than that the group kept a very low profile and were into a lot of legitimate business in the states – and that an inordinate number of the partners died in socalled "accidents" – not much. There was someone behind it who they couldn't find. Nobody was connected to the syndicates in the states in any way.

"Check on Donald Fielding. Him and Faith Richards, nee Faith Newsom. I think they're the two who came up with this insanity.

"Oh! You weren't in on that! I guess you know they've arrested Stedmann and charged him with murder."

"Judi told me. She said you were going to try to get him to say something. Did he?"

"Oh, yeah! Two or three somethings. At least three scumbags in Changuinola are going down on corruption charges. Fieldman is one of the starters of this game, if not the only starter. I have to find out what kind of relationship he and Newsom had going."

"Faith Richards lived with Stedmann for a short while in California. Carmel. Spent a lot of time in LA. Pretty well kept their noses clean. I'll check on Fieldman. LA?"

"Yeah. He's a genius control freak. I'll tell you about it when I see you."

"Fair enough. How are things, otherwise?"

They chatted for a few minutes, then Clint went to the computer and started searching for anything to do with the group, but particularly on Fieldman and Faith Richards.

He didn't find much about Fieldman. For someone as powerful as he was supposed to be, he kept off the net.

Money. He made damned sure he wasn't on any internet files. Probably used aliases for most of his deals.

Faith Richards. She was with Stedmann in LA for a couple of months in 1994, hot and heavy, then suddenly married Richards, a friend she met through a friend. Skinny was that she had an abortion a few days after they were married. They seemed to get along well and were in several businesses together. Richards introduced her to Fieldman. Interesting. 1997. She worked with him and her husband in a business deal and socialized a bit with him, but not much was known about it, only that the three went to dinners and theaters and such together about once a month. He had degrees in everything from psychology to business law. He had worked for a short period with an advisory and referral psychological clinic that specialized in schizophrenia and sociopathic personalities. There was no more than the fact he had worked there available. It didn't say what his specialty was or even if he had one. There was a short note that he was used on the relocation project (?). The group was formed in 1998.

Okay. Fieldman was the main manipulator. He had the resources and the knowledge. He could find members through some kind of relocation program. He could manipulate those kinds of people very well, thank you. People who lacked emotions could be conned into this kind of game. They felt nothing and spent their entire lives trying to find a way to experience an emotion. They could be very good at faking emotional responses. That was a survival trait.

How much of it was him alone and how much of it was from Faith Newsom being a master manipulator?

Clint had never met Faith Newsom. All he knew was that she was a knockout sex queen type who could act like an airhead, but who was actually far more than average intelligent.

He could meet her. It would have to be in Panamá City. Was that going to be necessary?

If he wanted some kind of clue to answer the questions it would.

He sighed and packed for the bus. He would be there in the morning, manage to meet the whole bunch there, then would, *maybe*, have an answer or two.

Clint slept on the bus. He got off for a few minutes at the Santiago terminal, used the rest room and got a decent meal, then went back to sleep when the bus started on the last half of the trip.

He got into Panamá City at a little after eleven and went to the Hotel California. He had, for once, had the sense to call and reserve a room. He went to the bar to talk with some people from Bocas Town, then turned in. Pancho told him where they were staying, the Hotel Europa, when he called to chat. He would manage to be in the restaurant at eight in the morning, which was when they always had breakfast. The Europa was only a couple of blocks away.

It was a pleasant enough night. Clint wondered about the world and how strange reality could be.

Here he was, involved with a bunch of certifiable lunatics running some kind of murder game and wasn't even kept awake by those facts for ten minutes. He knew how sick it was. Maybe he was a little short in the emotional part, himself – no. He felt very deeply about a lot of things and life was often exciting. He didn't need to search for what was wrong with him, though he knew damned well he had his own shortcomings.

Despite all that, he woke up very refreshed. He strolled around from five thirty, when he got out of bed, and ten 'til eight, when he went into the Europa's restaurant to order an omelet and a lot of coffee.

Clint had studied passport photos of most of them. They didn't show much, but enough that he could identify them. Harry and Faith Richards came in a few minutes before Gloria Stenson and Anne Haverton. Clint could see why she was always described as a knockout. She was, but in a slightly (deliberate) cheap way. Anne was rather pretty for a fifty-something woman, as was Gloria.

Donald Wentworth came in last and went to the table where Anne and Gloria were seated. He looked around the room and noticed Clint, who had spoken to him in the morgue in Changuinola. He nodded, said something to the women, then came over. Gloria had seen him when Donald pointed him out and had waved halfheartedly.

"Hello. Faraday, isn't it? We spoke a moment in that hospital thing? Donald Wentworth."

"Yes. I remember. I hope you aren't being too inconvenienced with this mess. I can't believe Stedmann thought he could get away with something like this. I came here to speak with him. He didn't have a whole to say, but we have most of the story about your group through the normal police methods."

"You find us strange, don't you?"

"People involved in that kind of game strange? Whatever gave you that idea!?"

He didn't react. He looked thoughtful, then, "So Mark told you about it?"

"No. He wouldn't. It's obvious as hell, when we start checking on you as a group. The blood trail is quite something. The pattern is blatant when you have enough facts on the table."

He nodded. "Stedmann was killing us off, I think. Maybe it was a game to him, but not to the rest of us."

"He wasn't even in Mexico for Truman and Smart or in Costa Rica for Stenson. That won't fly."

He looked a little uncertain. "Then more than one has to be behind it. Who do you think it is?"

"I said it won't fly. The ones in on it from the first, except maybe Fieldman (he looked like he'd been slapped when Clint used that name), who wasn't there for any of them, weren't there for some of the ten or so murders. Faith, Stedmann and Fieldman were the originators, but you all got into it with your eyes wide open. I imagine only a few wives or husbands or whatever could be ignorant of it. Maybe that's why Wanda had to go. She caught on.

"What happened? You were in Mexico, where Truman and Smart got wasted, and she began asking questions?"

He looked grim. He turned his back and went back to the table with Anne and Gloria. He got into an intense conversation with them. He soon went to the Richards' table to say something to them that included some arm waving. They looked over to see Clint unconcernedly eating his cheese omelet. Faith got up and came over. Harry came a few steps behind her.

"Hello. Clint Faraday isn't it? I'm Faith. Faith Richards.

"What is this conspiracy idea you told Donald about?"

"What theory? I didn't say anything about any conspiracy theory. I only said I knew a little about your game, that it's obvious when you have enough of the facts before you. I wondered if you were in on it with Fieldman or are just another person he was using.

"Actually, if you're in on it, you're being used. He's 'way out of your league.'"

She looked thoughtful. All of them had that one down pat. Clint wondered if it was an instinctive reaction or practiced.

"I've wondered about that myself. It was all a sort of mutual idea, I guess you'd say. Several of us, some who aren't here anymore, were in a group and wanted to find something to make a boring life a little exciting.

"Mr. Faraday, we don't ever bother anyone not in the group. That's always disaster!"

"Frank Carlysle was in the group? I don't think so."

"And it was a complete disaster. What he had was easily explainable as having something to do with a standard kind of doctor/patient confidentiality explanation. It could have been passed by as a fantasy, not a reality. That was what started the problems with the group.

"A man named Bernard and his wife were the cause of Carlysle's death. They're still around, so we fear them and try to avoid them."

"I see. They were responsible for Wanda Wentworth?"

"As I see it, yes. We're never sure. It makes the game a little more exciting. Mark was a fool to do anything that would make it plain who did what to whom."

"I see. You still think it's a matter among your group and no one else – even with the examples of

Carlysle and Wanda.”

“Wanda? What has that got to do with it?”

“She was never a member of your group. The police think Donald killed her because she found some very incriminating things.”

She studied him for a few seconds. They all seemed to have that one down pat, too.

“She was into blackmail.”

“I see. Only a total fool will try to blackmail a hit man.”

She let a grin escape. “How true.

“Are they going to let us go on soon? We haven’t done anything they can hold us for.”

“That’s up to them. They can hold you for as long as they like. This ain’t, as I explained to Stedmann, Texas.”

“I heard they don’t have to have a charge to hold you here. Guilty until proven innocent.”

“Not that. That works very well. The victim has rights here. They can hold you for investigation because of the connections with other murders in other places. Stedmann wasn’t there for the Mexico thing, so it’s, as you already suggested, conspiracy. They couldn’t care less about most conspiracies. When murder’s involved, they do.”

She nodded and said, “It’s been a pleasure, believe it or not. I could go for you in another time and another place.”

Clint gave her a short salute and they went back to

their tables.

It was Fieldman. He was sitting in Los Angeles manipulating, even here. Stedmann probably had a suggestion that he could get away with it. He knows he was set up, but that's just part of the game. Fieldman was untouchable. It was his invention. He was running the whole strange show through personality manipulation. It was something like a few of the horror shows on late night TV. Some nutcase causing all kinds of bloody mayhem while staying aloof from it. All of them were in a trap – but didn't care. Faith was ready enough to talk about it.

Why? Clint grinned to himself. He finished his breakfast and waved to the two tables, then went to the lobby to call Pancho. Pancho said he would get the information together for him as quickly as possible.

He waited, then got a call. It was what he thought was happening. "Faith Richards makes a call to Los Angeles, California, every morning at exactly two o'clock. She makes the call from the lobby telephone."

He thanked Pancho and said they could maybe take Faith Richards in for questioning. He called Sergio and asked what they could do. It wouldn't be possible to successfully prosecute any of them from here. Their part was almost all in other countries. The best they could do now was deport them back to the states.

Clint's thoughtful look was better and more sincere than that bunch. He said to let them know they were going to be deported to the states as soon as arrangements could be made through the American Embassy in Albrook. They would get the message in an hour or less when they would be picked up by the police.

"Clint? Might it not be a good idea to include Stedmann in that? We don't need the expense and aggravation of incarcerating such as him for the next twenty years."

"Might be interesting. Why not? They didn't do anything to anyone but themselves, here.

"Sergio, arrange for me to meet with them before they're taken out. Today or tomorrow. I want to get the hell out of Panamá City."

"Done."

"I just wanted to say a few things before you're packed back to the states," Clint said. The whole group, those still alive and in Panamá, were there in the interrogation room. They just stared at him and Faith pointed to the recorder.

Clint had it taken out of the room. He said they wouldn't need anything more to guarantee that the group never came near Panamá again. No one here needs the aggravation of dealing with a bunch of lunatics.

"Your word is totally inviolable. I've learned that much," Stedmann said. "Your word. You're not trying to get us to say something to pile on us."

"I'm going to explain what's been happening to you before you get back to the states. I guarantee you on my oath that we're not trying to get more from you. We have a hell of a lot more than we need. That's all. I don't think any of you know what's been happening to turn you into a pack of emotionless killers."

"Fire away!" Faith said. "I think I've finally figured out a lot of it. I've had too much time to think here. That opportunity didn't happen, so long as he could keep us in motion and in new places and situations. I'm not quite as stupid as I act. It's just easier if people think I'm a cheap bimbo with a lot of money and no sense."

"Uh-huh. You didn't use that act with me yesterday in the restaurant.

"Do you know what's happened? How you're all nothing but pawns for him to move or discard anyway he likes?"

"What the hell are you talking about?" Donald spat. "I'm no pawn for anybody!"

"We all are," Faith replied. "Let's hear what Faraday has to say. I know most of it, I think."

"Pawns? What ... Fieldman?" Stedmann asked.

"Exactly!" Anne cried. "I thought so! He's the only one we can't reach!"

"He may believe that," Stedmann said calmly. "Maybe he misses a little detail or two himself.

"Go on, Clint. I think maybe you aren't above a little manipulating of someone else's pawns, yourself."

"True," Clint agreed. "You can handle the situation the same way you were manipulated yourselves.

"Stedmann, you were with Faith before she married Harry, here. Harry introduced you to Fieldman, right?"

"No. I had a couple of sessions with him in a psychological group. Some other people were there. I had as much as forgotten that when Faith introduced me to him. I remembered the sessions and some other things that came up."

"Oh. He suggested you introduce them, Faith?"

She nodded. "Several of them. He would give me their names and how to sort of accidentally meet them in some place they went regularly."

"So it was a little earlier than I thought, but that doesn't really change anything. The point is that the meetings of everyone in the group was a manipulation by him for exactly what happened. He's been in control from the first. The real reason Carlysle is dead is not because of what was in the package, it was because something in that package connected him to you in a very dangerous, to him, way. He's running a sick game where he can cause you to kill off each other while he stays safe and sound in a house in LA. If they catch and prosecute all of you who are left he's still home free."

"Bastard son of a bitch!" Donald cried. "The slimy cocksucker stayed safe and put us all at each other!"

"He's not safe," Stedmann said. "He just thinks he is. He meant for me to be caught here, didn't he, Clint?"

"I think so. It's as effective a way as any other of taking you out of the game. He might have been a little scared of you, himself. You must have done or said something that would make him afraid he was going to lose control of you."

"I did. I asked him what the hell he thought he was doing in Costa Rica. Wanda wasn't part of the agreement. He sounded upset that I would question him at all."

"He knew you'd understand enough about the methods to stay alive and a danger to him, so he managed to get you out of the game another way.

"Faith, have you told him about being sent back to the states?"

"No. After breakfast yesterday, I wondered if that would be smart. I'm tired of actually being an idiot bimbo instead of just acting like one."

"Don't tell the stinking lousy bastard pig shit!" Donald ordered.

"Don't worry about *that!*?" she shot back.

"He made us into some kind of zombies, didn't he Mr. Faraday?" Gloria asked.

"That's a good description," Clint answered. "I think you should all find a way to protect yourselves when you get back. He's going to be desperate and he'll know something's wrong because Faith didn't make her regular call."

"I can call him now and explain that the police detained us again. I'll say I'll call again when I know what's up. I don't want him to know when I'm going to be back! He might have the plane shot down or something!"

Clint agreed and had a phone sent in. She said for no one to make a sound. She would act like she had sneaked away to call him from a public phone.

She called. The first thing she said when he answered was, "This has to be said fast. The cops are holding us all for questioning and they don't know I came out here. I think they're going to try to make us stay here until Mark's been convicted! It could be as much as ten days and I might not be able to get to a ... Uh-oh! He saw me! I've got to..." she hung up.

"Good show!" Stedmann said. "I think I've finally felt a little excitement!

"What now, Clint?"

"You go home. I'm out of it."

"You're a decent man," Gloria said. "If he knew ... we wouldn't stand a chance of being alive next week. I just *know* it!"

"So be very careful." Anne said. "I can get away. You can go with me. I've got some secrets he doesn't suspect.

"Faith, you and the guys are on your own. We couldn't work it with more than two and we were never in deep. That's what makes us dangerous. He'll think none of you can dare to talk. It'll mean you're hung by your own words. There's nothing to hang us with, except that we knew about it and were too scared to say anything."

"You were never scared of anything in your life!" Donald cried.

"You know that and I know that. They don't," she

said easily. "Thank you, Faraday. Maybe I have a trick or two up my sleeve that can shake the bastard."

An officer came to say that the man from the consulate was there to take them to the plane.

Clint got up and went home. Time would tell if he was as good at manipulating deficient psyches as Fieldman. He went back to David to spend a couple of days with friends. He would then go to Bocas Town and forget the detective business for as long as he could manage.

That was a sick bunch. He hoped he'd never have another case vaguely like it. Plain old everyday murders weren't a problem. This mess was. He still couldn't understand how anyone could be so empty as those people. It simply didn't, as said in the old TV show, calculate. Even when they were trying to find a way to keep from being killed by this maniac who manipulated them into becoming murderers themselves, they showed zilch as to emotions. It was all matter-of-fact and simply something they were discussing. It could have been about how pretty the sunset was last night and would show the same emptiness in them.

Not for Clint Faraday! Two of his Indio friends walked past Peter's Place in the Hotel Iris and waved. He felt a warm affection for them. If anything about an excess or lack of emotions applied to him it was on the excess end.

A pretty girl came to sit across the little table from him and start a conversation. So she was a prostitute. That was looked at in a different way here. He told her he had a girlfriend and wasn't interested. She nodded and said she wished she could trust her own boyfriends, but being in the business taught her that was true of one man out of a thousand.

"The thing is, it's a macho thing here. It's funny, but I think I find that the man who turns me down because he has honor is a lot more macho than the ones who just want to fuck and don't care who it's with. I'd offer a freebie, but you'd say `no,' right?"

Clint nodded. She laughed and insisted on buying him a drink. They talked a bit and she saw another gringo come in. A man in his sixties who looked around, then came to sit on the balcony four stools away.

"Back to business!" she said, gave him a peck on the cheek and went to talk to the gringo, who immediately waved for Yessie to bring her a drink. She winked at Clint and sat to lean close to talk to her new mark.

Clint grinned. He went to his room and to bed. He would go to Bocas in the morning. Chiriqui Grande and then home.

Clint laid back in the hammock on his deck to watch the CBS news from Denver. He'd been back for two days, the group of mixed nuts was back in the states and the case was marked as resolved by Sergio. That was the same as saying solved but not prosecuted here. It would serve very well.

Judi waved to him and went to water the orchids all over her deck and around her house. Dave had planted hundreds of varieties there (as well as at Clint's)(and at Ben's)(etc.) for study. The places were turning into small botanical gardens. Clint, despite himself, was getting interested in the amazing variety of forms, colors, and sizes. One was hanging on a limb about a meter from his head. It was a flower about 7cm across that was blooming on a plant that was no more than 2cm high!

Homalopetalum pumilio. He had even learned the scientific names of a few of them.

Suddenly, the girl telling a story about some homeless Colorado people having set fire to an old abandoned house and four of them had burned to death was handed a piece of paper.

"News Flash!" she said. "Just in from Los Angeles, California.

"Business magnate Donald Fieldman, owner of a national chain of hardware stores and eccentric recluse, has jumped from his twenty fourth floor balcony. Business partner Markus Stedmann, visiting at the time, says Fieldman was depressed about something and had excused himself to go to the sanitary. He had been gone for more than ten minutes when Stedmann went to look for him.

"Here is Vernon Vernon, on the scene."

The scene was in an alley with an ambulance and several police vehicles, including the CSI van.

"Thank you, Connie.

"It is too soon to make any positive statements, but it appears that Mr. Fieldman was depressed about some business failures that were having a domino effect on his holdings. The failures were in Central America, but were by the suppliers of much of the imported things sold in the Fieldman Enterprises stores. Mr. Stedmann, who admits that he was in some kind of legal trouble in one of those countries, said Mr. Fieldman was a bit intoxicated and deeply depressed. He suddenly said he must use the facilities and went from the room. About eight or ten minutes later, when he hadn't returned, Mr. Stedmann went to look for him, but could not find him in the apartment.

"Mr. Stedmann, in his statement to the police – that I was privy to – said that he noticed the balcony door was open. It wasn't when he went in because the air conditioner was on. He went out and found a scribbled message. It said, and I quote, `To the group: I have had enough of this shit. I want it to end. Now!' and was signed by Mr. Fieldman.

"That is about what we have to this point. Back to you, Connie."

"We will give more details as they come in. Now back to the report on the homeless ..."

Clint turned it off.

"I figured he would find a way. I wonder, did he feel any excitement when he dumped Fieldman off that balcony?"

He went back to the hammock with a Balboa to lay back and forget that bunch.

Another wonder: what happened to the rest of them? Would they continue the game on their own, now that they had no manipulator? Faith and Stedmann could get away with it. The others probably couldn't.

What a way to live!

Judi called across that she was going to the Nine Degrees for dinner. Did he want to go?

He thought about it.

Enough of restaurants for a while. He'd cook something himself.

"Thanks, but no thanks!" he called back.

Judi went inside and Clint laid back. The sunset across Saigon Bay was magnificent. The world has a lot to offer if you'll just see it – and no person or government is blinding you to it.

The computer dinged that it had e-mail.

"Screw it! Not tonight!" Clint decided.

C. D. Moultons works are available on most major outlets as printed or e-books. CD writes the CD Grimes, Pi mysteries, the Det. Lt. Nick Storie mysteries, the Clint Faraday mysteries, the Flight of the Maita science fiction series, books on orchid culture and many others of many types. Mystery, adventure, intrigue, science fiction, fantasy, paranormal, mild erotica, and factual.

www.ingramcontent.com/pod-product-compliance
Lightning Source LLC
Chambersburg PA
CBHW061619130726
47996CB00003B/1044